The Christopher Robin Collection

Tales of a Boy and his Bear

A. A. Milne

with decorations by E. H. Shepard

DRAWN BY ME

TO NORTH POLE

BEE TREE

BIG STONES AND ROX

RABBITS FRENDS AND RALETIONS

MY HOUSE

OWLS HOUSE

100 AKER WOOD

EEYORES GLOOMY PLACE

RATHER BOGGY AND SAD

ND MR SHEPARD HELPD

Contents

The Wrong Bees

(In which we are introduced to Winnie-the-Pooh
and some Bees, and the stories begin)

Here is Edward Bear,
coming downstairs now,

bump,
bump,
bump,

on the back of his head, behind Christopher Robin. It is,
as far as he knows, the only way of coming downstairs,
but sometimes he feels that there really is another way, if
only he could stop bumping for a moment and think of it.
And then he feels that perhaps there isn't. Anyhow, here
he is at the bottom, and ready to be introduced to you.
Winnie-the-Pooh.

When I first heard his name, I said, just as you are
going to say, 'But I thought he was a boy?'

'So did I,' said Christopher Robin.

'Then you can't call him Winnie?'

'I don't.'

'But you said –'

'He's Winnie-ther-Pooh. Don't you know what *"ther"* means?'

'Ah, yes, now I do,' I said quickly; and I hope you do too, because it is all the explanation you are going to get.

Sometimes Winnie-the-Pooh likes a game of some sort

when
   he
      comes
         downstairs,

and sometimes he likes to sit quietly in front of the fire and listen to a story. This evening –

'What about a story?' said Christopher Robin.

'*What* about a story?' I said.

'Could you very sweetly tell Winnie-the-Pooh one?'

'I suppose I could,' I said. 'What sort of stories does he like?'

'About himself. Because he's *that* sort of Bear.'

'Oh, I see.'

'So could you very sweetly?'
'I'll try,' I said. So I tried.

*   *   *

Once upon a time, a very long time ago now, about last Friday, Winnie-the-Pooh lived in a forest all by himself under the name of Sanders.

('What does "under the name" mean?' asked Christopher Robin.

'It means he had the name over the door in gold letters and lived under it.'

'Winnie-the-Pooh wasn't quite sure,' said Christopher Robin.

'Now I am,' said a growly voice.

'Then I will go on,' said I.)

One day when he was out walking, he came to an open place in the middle of the forest, and in the middle of this place was a large oak-tree, and, from the top of the tree,

3

there came a loud buzzing-noise.

Winnie-the-Pooh sat down at the foot of the tree, put his head between his paws, and began to think.

First of all he said to himself: 'That buzzing-noise means something. You don't get a buzzing-noise like that, just buzzing and buzzing, without its meaning something. If there's a buzzing-noise, somebody's making a buzzing-noise, and ...

... the only reason for making a buzzing-noise that I know of is because you're a bee.'

Then he thought another long time, and said:

'And the only reason for being a bee that I know of is making honey.'

And then he got up, and said:

'And the only reason for making honey is so as I can eat it.'

So he began to climb the tree.

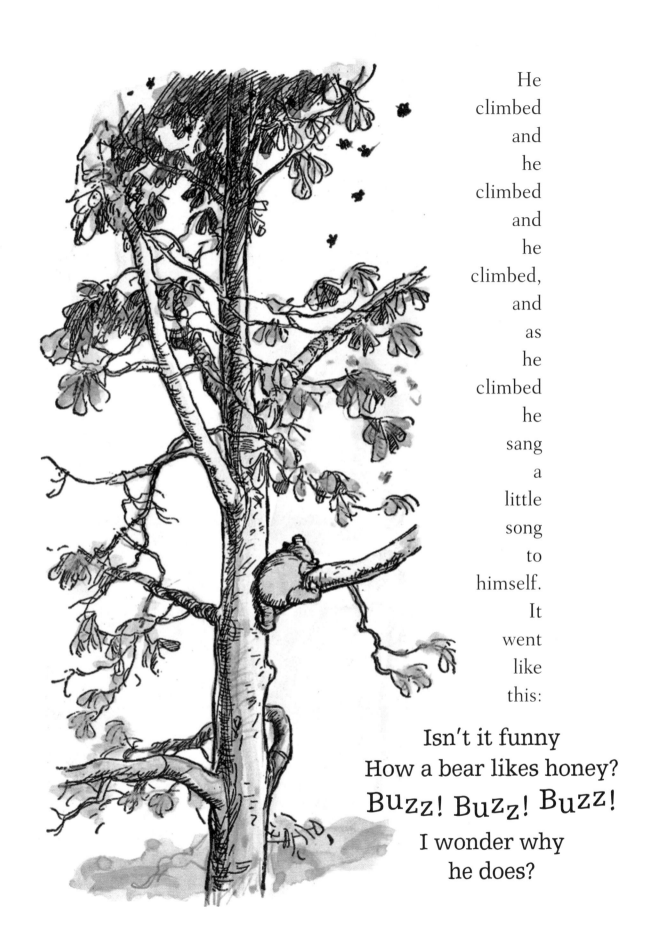

He
climbed
and
he
climbed
and
he
climbed,
and
as
he
climbed
he
sang
a
little
song
to
himself.
It
went
like
this:

Isn't it funny
How a bear likes honey?
Buzz! Buzz! Buzz!
I wonder why
he does?

Then he climbed a little further ... and a little further ... and then just a little further. By that time he had thought of another song.

It's a very funny thought that, if Bears were Bees,
They'd build their nests at the *bottom* of trees.
And that being so (if the Bees were Bears),
We shouldn't have to climb up all these stairs.

He was getting rather tired by this time, so that is why he sang a Complaining Song. He was nearly there now, and if he just stood on that branch ...

Crack!

'Oh, help!' said Pooh, as he dropped ten feet to the branch below him.

'If only I hadn't –' he said, as he bounced twenty feet on to the next branch.

'You see, what I *meant* to do,' he explained, as he turned head-over-heels, and crashed on to another branch thirty feet below,

'what I *meant* to do –'
'Of course, it *was* rather –' he admitted, as he slithered very quickly through the next six branches.

'It all comes, I suppose,' he decided, as he said good-bye to the last branch, spun round three times, and flew gracefully into a gorse-bush,

'it all comes of liking honey so much. Oh, help!'

He **crawled** out of the gorse-bush,

brushed the **prickles** from his **nose,** and
began to think again. And the first person he thought
of was Christopher Robin.

*('Was that me?' said Christopher Robin in an awed
voice, hardly daring to believe it.*

'That was you.'

*Christopher Robin said nothing, but his eyes got larger
and larger, and his face got pinker and pinker.)*

So Winnie-the-Pooh went round to his friend
Christopher Robin, who lived behind a green door in
another part of the Forest.

'Good morning, Christopher Robin,' he said.

'Good morning, Winnie-*ther*-Pooh,' said you.

'I wonder if you've got such a thing as a balloon about you?'

'A balloon?'

'Yes, I just said to myself coming along: "I wonder if Christopher Robin has such a thing as a balloon about him?" I just said it to myself, thinking of balloons, and wondering.'

'What do you want a balloon for?' you said.

Winnie-the-Pooh looked round to see that nobody was listening, put his paw to his mouth, and said in a deep whisper:

'Honey!'

'But you don't get honey with balloons!'

'*I* do,' said Pooh.

Well, it just happened that you had been to a party the day before at the house of your friend Piglet, and you had balloons at the party. You had had a big green balloon; and

10

one of Rabbit's relations had had a big blue one, and had left it behind, being really too young to go to a party at all; and so you had brought the green one *and* the blue one home with you.

'Which one would you like?' you asked Pooh.

He put his head between his paws and thought very carefully.

'It's like this,' he said. 'When you go after honey with a balloon, the great thing is not to let the bees know you're coming. Now, if you have a green balloon, they might think you were only part of the tree, and not notice you, and if you have a blue balloon, they might think you were only part of the sky, and not notice you, and the question is: Which is most likely?'

'Wouldn't they notice *you* underneath the balloon?' you asked.

'They might or they might not,' said Winnie-the-Pooh.

'You never can tell with bees.'

He thought for a moment and said: 'I shall try to look like a small black cloud. That will deceive them.'

'Then you had better have the blue balloon,' you said; and so it was decided.

Well, you both went out with the blue balloon, and you took your gun with you, just in case, as you always did, and Winnie-the-Pooh went to a very muddy place that he knew of, and **rolled** and **rolled**

until he was black all over;

and then, when the balloon was blown up as **big** as **big,** and you and Pooh were both holding on to the string, you let go suddenly, and Pooh Bear floated gracefully

up into the sky,

and stayed
there – level
with the top of the
tree and about twenty
feet away from it.

'Hooray!'

you shouted.

'Isn't that fine?' shouted Winnie-the-Pooh down to you.
'What do I look like?'

'You look like a bear holding on to a balloon,' you said.

'Not,' said Pooh anxiously, ' – not like a small black
cloud in a blue sky?'

'Not very much.'

'Ah, well, perhaps from up here it looks different.
And, as I say, you never can tell with bees.'

There was no wind to blow him nearer to the tree so
there he stayed. He could see the honey, he could smell
the honey, but he couldn't quite reach the honey.

After a little while he called down to you.

'Christopher Robin!' he said in a loud whisper.

'Hallo!'

'I think the bees *suspect* something!'

'What sort of thing?'

'I don't know. But something tells me that they're *suspicious*!'

'Perhaps they think that you're after their honey?'

'It may be that. **You never can tell with bees.**'

There was another little silence, and then he called down to you again.

'Christopher Robin!'

'Yes?'

'Have you an **umbrella** in your house?'

'I think so.'

'I wish you would bring it out here, and walk up and down with it, and look up at me every now and then, and say "Tut-tut, it looks like rain."

I think, if you did that, it would help the deception which we are practising on these bees.'

Well, you laughed to

yourself, **Silly old Bear!** but you didn't say it aloud because you were so fond of him, and you went home for your umbrella.

'Oh, there you are!' called down Winnie-the-Pooh, as soon as you got back to the tree. 'I was beginning to get anxious. I have discovered that the bees are now definitely Suspicious.'

'Shall I put my umbrella up?' you said.

'Yes, but wait a moment. We must be practical. The important bee to deceive is the Queen Bee. Can you see which is the Queen Bee from down there?'

'No.'

'A pity. Well, now, if you walk up and down with your umbrella, saying,

"Tut-tut, it looks like rain,"

I shall do what I can by singing a little Cloud Song, such as a cloud might sing . . . Go!'

So, while you walked up and down and wondered if it would rain, Winnie-the-Pooh sang this song:

How sweet to be a Cloud
Floating in the Blue!
Every little cloud
Always sings aloud.

How sweet to be a Cloud
Floating in the Blue!
It makes him very proud
To be a little cloud.

The bees were still buzzing as suspiciously as ever. Some of them, indeed, left their nests and flew all round the cloud as it began the second verse of this song, and one bee sat down on the nose of the cloud for a moment, and then got up again.

'Christopher – ow! – Robin,' called out the cloud.

'Yes?'

'I have just been thinking, and I have come to a very important decision. *These are the wrong sort of bees.*'

'Are they?'

'Quite the wrong sort. So I should think they would make the wrong sort of honey, shouldn't you?'

'Would they?'

'Yes.
So I
think
I shall
come
down.'

'How?' asked you.

Winnie-the-Pooh hadn't thought about this. If he let go of the string, he would fall –

bump

– and he didn't like the idea of that. So he thought for a long time, and then he said:

'Christopher Robin, you must shoot the balloon with your gun. Have you got your gun?'

'Of course I have,' you said. 'But if I do that, it will spoil the balloon,' you said.

'But if you *don't*,' said Pooh, 'I shall have to let go, and that would spoil *me*.'

When he put it like this, you saw how it was, and you aimed very carefully at the balloon, and fired.

'**Ow!**' said Pooh.

'Did I miss?' you asked.

'You didn't exactly *miss*,' said Pooh, 'but you missed the *balloon*.'

'I'm so sorry,' you said, and you fired again,

and this time you hit the balloon, and the air

came slowly out, and Winnie-the-Pooh

floated down to the ground.

But his arms were so stiff from
holding on to the string of the balloon all
that time that they stayed up straight in the air for
more than a week, and whenever a fly came and settled
on his nose he had to blow it off. And I think – but I am
not sure – that *that* is why he was always called Pooh.

'Is that the end of the story?' asked Christopher Robin.

'That's the end of that one. There are others.'

'About Pooh and Me?'

'And Piglet and Rabbit and all of you. Don't you remember?'

'I do remember, and then when I try to remember, I forget.'

'That day when Pooh and Piglet tried to catch the Heffalump –'

'They didn't catch it, did they?'

'No.'

'Pooh couldn't because he hasn't any brain. Did *I* catch it?'

'Well, that comes into the story.'

Christopher Robin nodded.

'I do remember,' he said, 'only Pooh doesn't very well, so that's why he likes having it told to him again. Because then it's a real story and not just a remembering.'

'That's just how *I* feel,' I said.

Christopher Robin gave a deep sigh, picked his Bear up by the leg, and walked off to the door, trailing Pooh behind him. At the door he turned and said, 'Coming to see me have my bath?'

20

'I might,' I said.

'I didn't hurt him when I shot him, did I?'

'Not a bit.'

He nodded and went out, and in a moment I heard Winnie-the-Pooh –

bump,

bump,

bump

– going up the stairs behind him.

Halfway Down

Halfway down the stairs
Is a stair
Where I sit.
There isn't any
Other stair
Quite like
It.
I'm not at the bottom,
I'm not at the top;
So this is the stair
Where
I always
Stop.

Halfway up the stairs
Isn't up,
And isn't down.
It isn't in the nursery,
It isn't in the town.
And all sorts of funny thoughts
Run round my head:
'It isn't really
Anywhere!
It's somewhere else
Instead!'

Buckingham Palace

They're changing guard at Buckingham Palace –
Christopher Robin went down with Alice.
Alice is marrying one of the guard.
   'A soldier's life is terrible hard,'
      Says Alice.

They're changing guard at Buckingham Palace –
Christopher Robin went down with Alice.
We saw a guard in a sentry-box.
   'One of the sergeants looks after their socks,'
      Says Alice.

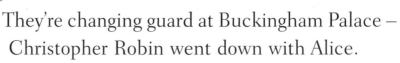

They're changing guard at Buckingham Palace –
Christopher Robin went down with Alice.
We looked for the King, but he never came.
'Well, God take care of him, all the same,'
                              Says Alice.

They're changing guard at Buckingham Palace –
Christopher Robin went down with Alice.
They've great big parties inside the grounds.
'I wouldn't be King for a hundred pounds,'
                              Says Alice.

They're changing guard at Buckingham Palace –
Christopher Robin went down with Alice.
A face looked out, but it wasn't the King's.
'He's much too busy a-signing things,'
                              Says Alice.

They're changing guard at Buckingham Palace –
Christopher Robin went down with Alice.
'Do you think the King knows all about *me*?'
'Sure to, dear, but it's time for tea,'
                              Says Alice.

The Woozle

(In which Pooh and Piglet go hunting and nearly catch a Woozle)

***

The piglet lived in a very grand house in the middle of a beech-tree, and the beech-tree was in the middle of the Forest, and the Piglet lived in the middle of the house. Next to his house was a piece of broken board which had:

TRESPASSERS W

on it. When Christopher Robin asked the Piglet what it meant, he said it was his grandfather's name, and had been in the family for a long time. Christopher Robin said you *couldn't* be called Trespassers W, and Piglet said yes, you could, because his grandfather was, and it was short for Trespassers Will, which was short for Trespassers William. And his grandfather had had two names in case he lost one – Trespassers after an uncle, and William after Trespassers.

26

'I've got two names,' said Christopher Robin carelessly.

'Well, there you are, that proves it,' said Piglet.

One fine winter's day when Piglet was brushing away the snow in front of his house, he happened to look up, and there was Winnie-the-Pooh. Pooh was walking round and round in a circle, thinking of something else,

and when Piglet called to him,
he just went on walking.

'Hallo!' said Piglet, 'what are *you* doing?'

'Hunting,' said Pooh.

'Hunting what?'

'Tracking something,' said Winnie-the-Pooh very mysteriously.

'Tracking what?' said Piglet, coming closer.

'That's just what I ask myself. I ask myself, What?'

'What do you think you'll answer?'

'I shall have to wait until I catch up with it,' said Winnie-the-Pooh. 'Now, look there.' He pointed to the ground in front of him. 'What do you see there?'

'Tracks,' said Piglet. 'Paw-marks.' He gave a little squeak of excitement, 'Oh, Pooh! Do you think it's a – a – a Woozle?'

29

'It may be,' said Pooh. 'Sometimes it is, and sometimes it isn't. You never can tell with paw-marks.'

With these few words he went on tracking, and Piglet, after watching him for a minute or two, ran after him. Winnie-the-Pooh had come to a sudden stop, and was bending over the tracks in a puzzled sort of way.

'What's the matter?' asked Piglet.

'It's a very funny thing,' said Bear, 'but there seem to be *two* animals now. This – whatever-it-is – has been joined by another – whatever-it-is – and the two of them are now proceeding in company. Would you mind coming with me, Piglet, in case they turn out to be Hostile Animals?'

Piglet scratched his ear in a nice sort of way, and said that he had nothing to do until Friday, and would be delighted to come, in case it really *was* a **Woozle.**

'You mean, in case it really is **two Woozles,'** said Winnie-the-Pooh, and Piglet said that anyhow he had nothing to do until Friday. So off they went together.

There was a small spinney of larch-trees just here, and it seemed as if the two Woozles, if that is what they were, had been going round this spinney; so round this spinney went Pooh and Piglet after them; Piglet passing the time by telling Pooh what his grandfather Trespassers W had done to Remove Stiffness after Tracking, and how his grandfather Trespassers W had suffered in his later years from Shortness of Breath, and other matters of interest, and Pooh wondering what a grandfather was like, and if perhaps

this was Two Grandfathers they were after now, and, if so, whether he would be allowed to take one home and keep it, and what Christopher Robin would say. And still the tracks went on in front of them . . .

Suddenly Winnie-the-Pooh stopped, and pointed excitedly in front of him. *'Look!'*

'What?' said Piglet, with a j**u**mp. And then, to show that he hadn't been frightened, he jumped **up** and **down** once or twice more in an exercising sort of way.

'The tracks!' said Pooh. 'A *third animal has joined the other two!*'

'Pooh!' cried Piglet. 'Do you think it is another Woozle?'

'No,' said Pooh, 'because it makes different marks. It is either **Two Woozles** and one, as it might be, **Wizzle,** or **Two,** as it might be, **Wizzles** and **one,** if so it is, **Woozle.** Let us continue to follow them.'

So they went on, feeling just a little anxious now, in case the three animals in front of them were of Hostile Intent. And Piglet wished very much that his grandfather T. W. were there, instead of elsewhere, and Pooh thought how nice it would be if they met Christopher Robin suddenly but quite accidentally, and only because he liked Christopher Robin so much. And then, all of a

sudden, Winnie-the-Pooh stopped again, and licked the tip of his nose in a cooling manner, for he was feeling more hot and anxious than ever in his life before. *There were* **four** *animals in front of them!*

'Do you see, Piglet? Look at their tracks! **Three,** as it were, **Woozles,** and **one,** as it was, **Wizzle.** *Another* **Woozle** *has joined them!'*

And so it seemed to be. There were the tracks; crossing over each other here, getting muddled up with each other there; but, quite plainly every now and then, the tracks of four sets of paws.

'I *think*,' said Piglet, when he had licked the tip of his nose too, and found that it brought very little comfort, 'I *think* that I have just remembered something. I have just

remembered something that I forgot to do yesterday and shan't be able to do to-morrow. So I suppose I really ought to go back and do it now.'

'We'll do it this afternoon, and I'll come with you,' said Pooh.

'It isn't the sort of thing you can do in the afternoon,' said Piglet quickly. 'It's a very particular morning thing, that has to be done in the morning, and, if possible, between the hours of – What would you say the time was?'

'About twelve,' said Winnie-the-Pooh, looking at the sun.

'Between, as I was saying, the hours of twelve and twelve five. So, really, dear old Pooh, if you'll excuse me – *What's that?*'

Pooh looked up at the sky, and then, as he heard the whistle again, he looked up into the branches of a big oak-tree, and then he saw a friend of his.

'It's **Christopher Robin,**' he said.

'Ah, then you'll be all right,' said Piglet. 'You'll be quite safe with *him*. Good-bye,' and he trotted off home as quickly as he could, very glad to be Out of All Danger again. Christopher Robin came slowly down his tree.

'Silly old Bear,' he said, 'what *were* you doing? First you went round the spinney twice by yourself, and then Piglet ran after you and you went round again together, and then you were just going round a fourth time –'

'Wait a moment,' said Winnie-the-Pooh, holding up his paw.

He sat down and thought, in the most thoughtful way he could think. Then he fitted his paw into one of the tracks . . . and then he scratched his nose twice, and stood up.

'Yes,' said Winnie-the-Pooh.

'I see now,' said Winnie-the-Pooh.

'I have been **Foolish** and **Deluded,**' said he, 'and I am a Bear of No Brain at All.'

'You're the Best Bear in All the World,' said Christopher Robin soothingly.

'Am I?' said Pooh hopefully. And then he brightened up suddenly.

'Anyhow,' he said, 'it is nearly Luncheon Time.'

So he went home for it.

The North Pole

(In which Christopher Robin
leads an expotition to the North Pole)

• • • • • • • • • • • • • • • • • •

One fine day Pooh had stumped up to the top of the Forest to see if his friend Christopher Robin was interested in Bears at all. At breakfast that morning (a simple meal of marmalade spread lightly over a honeycomb or two) he had suddenly thought of a new song. It began like this:

'Sing Ho! for the life of a Bear.'

When he had got as far as this, he scratched his head, and thought to himself, 'That's a very good start for a song, but what about the second line?' He tried singing 'Ho,' two or three times, but it didn't seem to help. 'Perhaps it would be better,' he thought, 'if I sang Hi for the life of a Bear.' So he sang it . . . but it wasn't. 'Very well then,' he said, 'I shall sing that first line twice,

38

and perhaps if I sing it very quickly, I shall find myself singing the third and fourth lines before I have time to think of them, and that will be a Good Song. Now then:'

Sing Ho! for the life of a Bear!
Sing Ho! for the life of a Bear!
I don't much mind if it rains or snows,
'Cos I've got a lot of honey on my nice new nose!
I don't much care if it snows or thaws,
'Cos I've got a lot of honey on my nice clean paws!
Sing Ho! for a Bear!
Sing Ho! for a Pooh!
And I'll have a little something in an hour or two!

He was so pleased with this song that he sang it all the way to the top of the Forest, 'and if I go on singing it much longer,' he thought, 'it will be time for the little something, and then the last line won't be true.' So he turned it into a hum instead.

Christopher Robin was sitting outside his door, putting on his **Big** Boots.

As soon as he saw the **Big** Boots, Pooh knew that an **Adventure** was going to happen, and he brushed the honey off his nose with the back of his paw, and spruced himself up as well as he could, so as to look **Ready for Anything.**

'Good morning, Christopher Robin,' he called out.

'Hallo, Pooh Bear. I can't get this boot on.'

'That's bad,' said Pooh.

'Do you think you could very kindly lean against me, 'cos I keep pulling so hard that I fall over backwards.'

Pooh sat down, dug his feet into the ground, and **pushed** hard against Christopher Robin's back, and Christopher Robin **pushed** hard against his, and **pulled** and **pulled** at his boot until he had got it on.

'And that's that,' said Pooh. 'What do we do next?'

'We are all going on an Expedition,'

said Christopher Robin, as he got up and brushed himself. 'Thank you, Pooh.'

'Going on an **Expotition?**' said Pooh eagerly. 'I don't think I've ever been on one of those. Where are we going to on this **Expotition?**'

'Expedition, silly old Bear. It's got an "x" in it.'

'Oh!' said Pooh. 'I know.' But he didn't really.

'We're going to discover the North Pole.'

'Oh!' said Pooh again. 'What *is* the North Pole?' he asked.

'It's just a thing you discover,' said Christopher Robin carelessly, not being quite sure himself.

'Oh! I see,' said Pooh. 'Are bears any good at discovering it?'

'Of course they are. And Rabbit and Kanga and all of you. It's an Expedition. That's what an Expedition means. A long line of everybody. You'd better tell the others to get ready, while I see if my gun's all right. And we must all bring Provisions.'

'Bring what?'

'Things to eat.'

'Oh!' said Pooh happily. 'I thought you said Provisions. I'll go and tell them.' And he stumped off.

The first person he met was Rabbit.

'Hallo, Rabbit,' he said, 'is that you?'

'Let's pretend it isn't,' said Rabbit, 'and see what happens.'

'I've got a message for you.'

'I'll give it to him.'

'We're all going on an Ex**potition** with Christopher Robin!'

'What is it when we're on it?'

'A sort of boat, I think,' said Pooh.

'Oh! that sort.'

'Yes. And we're going to discover a Pole or something.

Or was it a Mole?

Anyhow we're going to discover it.'

'We are, are we?' said Rabbit.

'Yes. And we've got to bring Pro-things to eat with us. In case we want to eat them. Now I'm going down to Piglet's. Tell Kanga, will you?'

He left Rabbit and hurried down to Piglet's house. The Piglet was sitting on the ground at the door of his house blowing happily at a dandelion, and wondering whether

it would be this year, next year, sometime, or never. He had just discovered that it would be never, and was trying to remember what '*it*' was, and hoping it wasn't anything nice, when Pooh came up.

'Oh! Piglet,' said Pooh excitedly, **'we're going on an Expotition, all of us, with things to eat.** To discover something.'

'To discover what?' said Piglet anxiously.

'Oh! just something.'

'Nothing fierce?'

'Christopher Robin didn't say anything about fierce. He just said it had an "x".'

'It isn't their **necks** I mind,' said Piglet earnestly. 'It's their **teeth.** But if Christopher Robin is coming I don't mind anything.'

In a little while they were all ready at the top of the Forest, and the Expotition started.

First came Christopher Robin and Rabbit, then Piglet and Pooh; then Kanga, with Roo in her pocket, and Owl; then Eeyore; and, at the end, in a long line, all Rabbit's friends-and-relations.

'I didn't ask them,' explained Rabbit carelessly. 'They just came. They always do. They can march at the end, after Eeyore.'

'What I say,' said Eeyore, 'is that it's unsettling. I didn't want to come on this Expo – what Pooh said. I only came to oblige. But here I am; and if I am the end of the Expo – what we're talking about – then let me *be* the end. But if, every time I want to sit down for a little rest, I have to brush away half a dozen of Rabbit's smaller friends-and-relations first, then this isn't an Expo – whatever it is – at all, it's simply a **Confused Noise.** That's what *I* say.'

'I see what Eeyore means,' said Owl. 'If
you ask me –'

'I'm not asking anybody,' said Eeyore. 'I'm
just telling everybody. We can look for the North
Pole, or we can play "Here we go gathering Nuts
and May" with the end part of an ants' nest. It's all the
same to me.'

There was a shout from the top of the line.

'**Come on!**' called Christopher Robin.

'**Come on!**' called Pooh and Piglet.

'**Come on!**' called Owl.

'We're starting,' said Rabbit. 'I must go.' And he hurried
off to the front of the Expotition with Christopher Robin.

'All right,' said Eeyore. 'We're going.
Only Don't Blame Me.'

So off they all went to discover the Pole. And as they
walked, they chattered to each other of this and that, all
except Pooh, who was making up a song.

'This is the first verse,' he said to Piglet, when he was
ready with it.

'First verse of what?'

'My song.'

'What song?'

'This one.'

'Which one?'

'Well, if you listen, Piglet, you'll hear it.'

'How do you know I'm not listening?'

Pooh couldn't answer that one, so he began to sing.

They all went off to discover the Pole,

Owl and Piglet and Rabbit and all;

It's a Thing you Discover, as I've been tole

By Owl and Piglet and Rabbit and all.

Eeyore, Christopher Robin and Pooh

And Rabbit's relations all went too –

And where the Pole was none of them knew . . .

Sing Hey! for Owl and Rabbit and all!

'Hush!' said Christopher Robin, turning round to Pooh, 'we're just coming to a Dangerous Place.'

'Hush!' said Pooh, turning round quickly to Piglet.

'Hush!' said Piglet to Kanga.

'Hush!' said Kanga to Owl, while Roo said 'Hush!' several times to himself very quietly.

'Hush!' said Owl to Eeyore.

'Hush!' said Eeyore in a terrible voice to all Rabbit's friends-and-relations, and 'Hush!' they said hastily to each other all down the line, until it got to the last one of all. And the last and smallest friend-and-relation was so upset to find that the whole Expotition was saying 'Hush!' to *him*, that he buried himself head downwards in a crack in the ground, and stayed there for two days until the danger was over, and then went home in a great hurry, and lived quietly with his Aunt ever-afterwards. His name was Alexander Beetle.

They had come to a stream which twisted and tumbled between high rocky banks, and Christopher Robin saw at once how dangerous it was.

'It's just the place,' he explained, 'for an **Ambush.'**

'What sort of bush?' whispered Pooh to Piglet. 'A gorse-bush?'

'My dear Pooh,' said Owl in his superior way, 'don't you know what an Ambush is?'

'Owl,' said Piglet, looking round at him severely, 'Pooh's whisper was a perfectly private whisper, and there was no need –'

'An **Ambush,'** said Owl, 'is a sort of **Surprise.'**

'So is a gorse-bush sometimes,' said Pooh.

'An Ambush, as I was about to explain to Pooh,' said Piglet, 'is a sort of Surprise.'

'If people jump out at you suddenly, that's an Ambush,' said Owl.

'It's an Ambush, Pooh, when people jump at you suddenly,' explained Piglet.

Pooh, who now knew what an Ambush was, said that a gorse-bush had sprung at him suddenly one day when he fell off a tree, and he had taken six days to get all the prickles out of himself.

'We are not *talking* about gorse-bushes,' said Owl a little crossly.

'I am,' said Pooh.

They were climbing very cautiously up the stream now, going from rock to rock, and after they had gone a little way they came to a place where the banks widened out at each side, so that on each side of the water there was a level strip of grass on which they could sit down and rest. As soon as he saw this, Christopher Robin called

'Halt!'

and they all sat down and rested.

'I think,' said Christopher Robin, 'that we ought to eat all our Provisions now, so that we shan't have so much to carry.'

'Eat all our what?' said Pooh.

'All that we've brought,' said Piglet, getting to work.

'That's a good idea,' said Pooh, and he got to work too.

'Have you all got something?' asked Christopher Robin with his mouth full.

'All except me,' said Eeyore. 'As Usual.' He looked round at them in his melancholy way. 'I suppose none of you are sitting on a thistle by any chance?'

'I believe I am,' said Pooh. 'Ow!' He got up, and looked behind him. 'Yes, I was. I thought so.'

'Thank you, Pooh. If you've quite finished with it.' He moved across to Pooh's place, and began to eat.

'It doesn't do them any Good, you know, sitting on them,' he went on, as he looked up munching. 'Takes all the Life out of them. Remember that another time, all of you.

A little Consideration, a little Thought for Others, makes all the difference.'

As soon as he had finished his lunch Christopher Robin whispered to Rabbit, and Rabbit said, 'Yes, yes, of course,' and they walked a little way up the stream together.

'I didn't want the others to hear,' said Christopher Robin.

'Quite so,' said Rabbit, looking important.

'It's – I wondered – It's only – Rabbit, I suppose *you* don't know. What does the North Pole *look* like?'

'Well,' said Rabbit, stroking his whiskers, 'now you're asking me.'

'I did know once, only I've sort of forgotten,' said Christopher Robin carelessly.

'It's a funny thing,' said Rabbit, 'but I've sort of forgotten too, although I did know *once*.'

'I suppose it's just a pole stuck in the ground?'

'Sure to be a pole,' said Rabbit, 'because of calling it a pole, and if it's a pole, well, I should think it would be sticking in the ground, shouldn't you, because there'd be nowhere else to stick it.'

'Yes, that's what I thought.'

'The only thing,' said Rabbit, 'is, *where is it sticking?*'

'That's what we're looking for,' said Christopher Robin.

They went back to the others. Piglet was lying on his

back, sleeping peacefully. Roo was washing his face and paws in the stream, while Kanga explained to everybody proudly that this was the first time he had ever washed his face himself, and Owl was telling Kanga an Interesting Anecdote full of long words like Encyclopædia and Rhododendron to which Kanga wasn't listening.

'I don't hold with all this washing,' grumbled Eeyore. 'This modern Behind-the-ears nonsense. What do *you* think, Pooh?'

'Well,' said Pooh, '*I* think –'

But we shall never know what Pooh thought, for there came a sudden **squeak** from Roo, a **splash,** and a loud cry of alarm from Kanga.

'So much for *washing,'* said Eeyore.

'Roo's fallen in!'

cried Rabbit, and he and Christopher Robin came rushing down to the rescue.

'Look at me swimming!' squeaked Roo from the middle of his pool, and was hurried down a waterfall into the next pool.

'Are you all right, Roo dear?' called Kanga anxiously.

'Yes!' said Roo. **'Look at me sw–'** and down he went

54

over the next waterfall into another pool.

Everybody was doing something to help. Piglet, wide awake suddenly, was jumping up and down and making 'Oo, I say' noises; Owl was explaining that in a case of Sudden and Temporary Immersion the Important Thing was to keep the Head Above Water; Kanga was jumping along the bank, saying, 'Are you *sure* you're all right, Roo dear?' to which Roo, from whatever pool he was in at the moment, was answering, 'Look at me swimming!'

Eeyore had turned round and hung his tail over the first pool into which Roo fell, and with his back to the accident was grumbling quietly to himself, and saying, 'All this washing; but catch on to my tail, little Roo, and you'll be all right'; and Christopher Robin and Rabbit came hurrying past Eeyore, and were calling out to the others in front of them.

'All right, Roo, I'm coming,' called Christopher Robin.

'Get something across the stream lower down, some of you fellows,' called Rabbit.

But Pooh was getting something. Two pools below Roo he was standing with a long pole in his paws, and Kanga came up and took one end of it, and between them they held it across the lower part of the pool; and Roo, still bubbling proudly, **'Look at me swimming,'** drifted up against it, and climbed out.

'Did you see me swimming?' squeaked Roo excitedly, while Kanga scolded him and rubbed him down. 'Pooh, did you see me swimming? That's called swimming, what I was doing. Rabbit, did you see what I was doing? Swimming. Hallo, Piglet! I say, Piglet! What do you think I was doing! Swimming! Christopher Robin, did you see me –'

But Christopher Robin wasn't listening. He was looking at Pooh.

'Pooh,' he said, 'where did you find that pole?'

Pooh looked at the pole in his hands.

'I just found it,' he said. 'I thought it ought to be useful. I just picked it up.'

'Pooh,' said Christopher Robin solemnly, 'the Expedition is over. You have found the North Pole!'

'Oh!' said Pooh.

Eeyore was sitting with his tail in the water when they all got back to him.

'Tell Roo to be quick, somebody,' he said. 'My tail's getting cold. I don't want to mention it, but I just mention it. I don't want to complain, but there it is. My tail's cold.'

'Here I am!' squeaked Roo.

'Oh, there you are.'

'Did you see me swimming?'

Eeyore took his tail out of the water, and swished it from side to side.

'As I expected,' he said. 'Lost all feeling. Numbed it. That's what it's done. Numbed it. Well, as long as nobody minds, I suppose it's all right.'

'Poor old Eeyore! I'll dry it for you,' said Christopher Robin, and he took out his handkerchief and rubbed it up.

'Thank you, Christopher Robin. You're the only one

who seems to understand about tails. They don't think – that's what's the matter with some of these others. They've no imagination.

A tail isn't a tail to them, it's just a Little Bit Extra at the back.'

'Never mind, Eeyore,' said Christopher Robin, rubbing his hardest. 'Is *that* better?'

'It's feeling more like a tail perhaps.

It Belongs again, if you know what I mean.'

'Hullo, Eeyore,' said Pooh, coming up to them with his pole.

'Hullo, Pooh. Thank you for asking, but I shall be able to use it again in a day or two.'

'Use what?' said Pooh.

'What we are talking about.'

'I wasn't talking about anything,' said Pooh, looking puzzled.

'My mistake again. I thought you were saying how sorry you were about my tail, being all numb, and could you do anything to help?'

'No,' said Pooh. 'That wasn't me,' he said. He thought for a little and then suggested helpfully: 'Perhaps it was somebody else.'

'Well, thank him for me when you see him.'

Pooh looked anxiously at Christopher Robin.

'Pooh's found the North Pole,' said Christopher Robin. 'Isn't that lovely?'

Pooh looked modestly down.

'Is that it?' said Eeyore.

'Yes,' said Christopher Robin.

'Is that what we were looking for?'

'Yes,' said Pooh.

'Oh!' said Eeyore. 'Well, anyhow – it didn't rain,' he said.

They stuck the pole in the ground, and Christopher Robin tied a message on to it:

NorTH PoLE
DICSovERED By
PooH
PooH FouND IT

Then they all went home again. And I think, but I am not quite sure, that Roo had a hot bath and went straight to bed. But Pooh went back to his own house, and feeling very proud of what he had done, had a little something to revive himself.

Sand-Between-the-Toes

I went down to the shouting sea,
Taking Christopher down with me,
For Nurse had given us sixpence each –
And down we went to the beach.

We had sand in the eyes and the ears and the nose,
And sand in the hair, and sand-between-the-toes.

64

Whenever a good nor'-wester blows,
Christopher is certain of
Sand-between-the-toes.

The sea was galloping grey and white;
Christopher clutched his sixpence tight;
We clambered over the humping sand –
And Christopher held my hand.

We had sand in the eyes and the ears and the nose,
And sand in the hair, and sand-between-the-toes.
Whenever a good nor'-wester blows,
Christopher is certain of
Sand-between-the-toes.

There was a roaring in the sky;
The sea-gulls cried as they blew by,
We tried to talk, but had to shout –
Nobody else was out.

When we got home, we had sand in the hair,
In the eyes and the ears and everywhere;
Whenever a good nor'-wester blows,
Christopher is found with
Sand-between-the-toes.

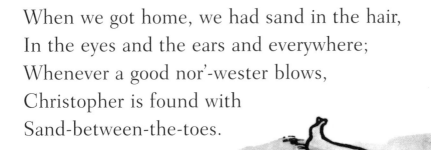

We Say Goodbye

(In which Christopher Robin
gives a Pooh Party, and we say good-bye)

One day when the sun had come back over the Forest, bringing with it the scent of may, and all the streams of the Forest were tinkling happily to find themselves their own pretty shape again, and the little pools lay dreaming of the life they had seen and the big things they had done, and in the warmth and quiet of the Forest the cuckoo was trying over his voice carefully and listening to see if he liked it, and wood-pigeons were complaining gently to themselves in their lazy comfortable way that it was the other fellow's fault, but it didn't matter very much; on such a day as this Christopher Robin whistled in a special way he had, and Owl came flying out of the Hundred Acre Wood to see what was wanted.

'Owl,' said Christopher Robin,

'I am going to give a party.'

'You are, are you?' said Owl.

'And it's to be a special sort of party, because it's because of what Pooh did when he did what he did to save Piglet from the flood.'

'Oh, that's what it's for, is it?' said Owl.

'Yes, so will you tell Pooh as quickly as you can, and all the others, because it will be to-morrow?'

'Oh, it will, will it?' said Owl, still being as helpful as possible.

'So will you go and tell them, Owl?'

Owl tried to think of something very wise to say, but couldn't, so he flew off to tell the others. And the first person he told was Pooh.

'Pooh,' he said. 'Christopher Robin is giving a party.'

'Oh!' said Pooh. And then seeing that Owl expected him to say something else, he said, 'Will there be those little cake things with pink sugar icing?'

Owl felt that it was rather beneath him to talk

about little cake things with pink sugar icing, so he told Pooh exactly what Christopher Robin had said, and flew off to Eeyore.

'A party for Me?' thought Pooh to himself. 'How grand!'

And he began to wonder if all the other animals would know that it was a special Pooh Party, and if Christopher Robin had told them about *The Floating Bear* and *The Brain of Pooh* and all the wonderful ships he had invented and sailed on, and he began to think how awful it would be if everybody had forgotten about it, and nobody quite knew what the party was for; and the more he thought like this, the more the party got muddled in his mind, like a dream when nothing goes right. And the dream began to sing itself over in his head until it became a sort of song. It was an ...

ANXIOUS POOH SONG

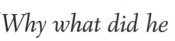
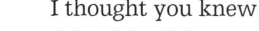
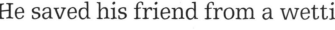

3 Cheers for Pooh!
(For who?)
For Pooh –
(Why what did he do?)
I thought you knew;
He saved his friend from a wetting!
3 Cheers for Bear!
(For where?)
For Bear –
He couldn't swim,
But he rescued him!
(He rescued who?)
Oh, listen, do!
I am talking of Pooh –
(Of who?)
Of Pooh!
(I'm sorry I keep forgetting.)
Well, Pooh was a Bear of Enormous Brain –
(Just say it again!)

Of enormous brain –
(*Of enormous what?*)
Well, he ate a lot,
And I don't know if he could swim or not,
But he managed to float
On a sort of boat
(*On a sort of what?*)
Well, a sort of pot –
So now let's give him three hearty cheers
(*So now let's give him three hearty whiches?*)
And hope he'll be with us for years and years,
And grow in health and wisdom and riches!
3 Cheers for Pooh!
(*For who?*)
For Pooh – 
3 Cheers for Bear!
(*For where?*)
For Bear –
3 Cheers for the wonderful Winnie-the-Pooh!
(*Just tell me, somebody – WHAT DID HE DO?*)

While this was
going on inside him,
Owl was talking to
Eeyore.

'Eeyore,' said Owl,
'Christopher Robin is
giving a party.'

'Very interesting,' said
Eeyore. 'I suppose they will be sending me down the odd
bits which got trodden on.

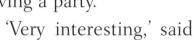

Kind and Thoughtful. Not at all, don't mention it.'

'There is an Invitation for you.'
'What's that like?'
'An Invitation!'
'Yes, I heard you. Who dropped it?'

'This isn't anything to eat, it's asking
you to the party. To-morrow.'

Eeyore shook his head
slowly.

'You mean Piglet. The

little fellow with the excited ears. That's Piglet. I'll tell him.'

'No, no,' said Owl, getting quite fussy. 'It's you!'

'Are you sure?'

'Of course I'm sure. Christopher Robin said "All of them! Tell all of them."'

'All of them, except Eeyore?'

'All of them,' said Owl sulkily.

'Ah!' said Eeyore. 'A mistake, no doubt, but still, I shall come. Only don't blame me if it rains.'

But it didn't rain. Christopher Robin had made a long table out of some long pieces of wood, and they all sat round it. Christopher Robin sat at one end, and Pooh sat at the other, and between them on one side were Owl and Eeyore and Piglet, and between them on the other side were Rabbit and Roo and Kanga. And all Rabbit's friends and relations spread themselves about on the grass, and waited hopefully in case anybody spoke to them, or dropped anything, or asked them the time.

It was the first party to which Roo had ever been, and he was very excited. As soon as ever they had sat down he began to talk.

'Hallo, Pooh!' he squeaked.

'Hallo, Roo!' said Pooh.

Roo jumped up and down in his seat for a little while and then began again.

'Hallo, Piglet!' he squeaked.

Piglet waved a paw at him, being too busy to say anything.

'Hallo, Eeyore!' said Roo.

Eeyore nodded gloomily at him. 'It will rain soon, you see if it doesn't,' he said.

Roo looked to see if it didn't, and it didn't, so he said,

'Hallo, Owl!'

– and Owl said, 'Hallo, my little fellow,' in a kindly way, and went on telling Christopher Robin about an accident

which had nearly happened to a friend of his whom Christopher Robin didn't know, and Kanga said to Roo, 'Drink up your milk first, dear, and talk afterwards.' So Roo, who was drinking his milk, tried to say that he could do both at once . . . and had to be patted on the back and dried for quite a long time afterwards.

When they had all nearly eaten enough, Christopher Robin banged on the table with his spoon, and everybody stopped talking and was very silent, except Roo who was just finishing a loud attack of hiccups and trying to look as if it was one of Rabbit's relations.

'This party,' said Christopher Robin, 'is a party because of what someone did, and we all know who it was, and it's his party, because of what he did, and I've got a present for him and here it is.' Then he felt about a little and whispered, 'Where is it?'

While he was looking, Eeyore coughed in an impressive way and began to speak.

'Friends,' he said, 'including oddments, it is a great pleasure, or perhaps I had better say it has been a pleasure so far, to see you at my party. What I did was nothing. Any of you – except Rabbit and Owl and Kanga – would have done the same. Oh, and Pooh. My remarks do not, of course, apply to Piglet and Roo, because they are too small. Any of you would have done the same. But it just happened to be Me. It was not, I need hardly say, with an idea of getting what Christopher Robin is looking for now' – and he put his front leg to his mouth and said in a loud whisper, 'Try under the table' – 'that I did what I did – but because I feel that we should all do what we can to help. I feel that we should all –'

'H-h^up!' said Roo accidentally.

'Roo, dear!' said Kanga reproachfully.

'Was it me?' asked Roo, a little surprised.

'What's Eeyore talking about?' Piglet whispered to Pooh.

'I don't know,' said Pooh rather dolefully.

'I thought this was *your* party.'

'I thought it was *once*. But I suppose it isn't.'

'I'd sooner it was yours than Eeyore's,' said Piglet.

'So would I,' said Pooh.

'H-hup!' said Roo again.

'AS – I – WAS – SAYING,'

said Eeyore loudly and sternly, 'as I was saying when I was interrupted by various Loud Sounds, I feel that –'

'Here it is!' cried Christopher Robin excitedly. 'Pass it down to silly old Pooh. It's for Pooh.'

'For Pooh?' said Eeyore.

'Of course it is.

The best bear in all the world.'

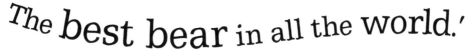

'I might have known,' said Eeyore. 'After all, one can't complain. I have my friends. Somebody spoke to me only yesterday. And was it last week or the week before that Rabbit bumped into me and said, "Bother!" The Social Round. Always something going on.'

Nobody was listening, for they were all saying,

'Open it, Pooh,'

'What is it, Pooh?'

'I know what it *is*,'

'No, you don't,'

and other helpful remarks of this sort. And of course Pooh was opening it as quickly as ever he could, but without cutting the string, because you never know when a bit of string might be Useful. At last it was undone.

When Pooh saw what it was, he nearly fell down, he was so pleased.

It was a Special Pencil Case. There were pencils in it marked 'B' for Bear, and pencils marked 'HB' for Helping Bear, and pencils marked 'BB' for Brave Bear.

There was a knife for sharpening the pencils, and an india rubber for rubbing out anything which you had spelt wrong, and a ruler for ruling lines for the words to walk on, and inches marked on the ruler in case you wanted to know how many inches anything was, and **Blue Pencils** and **Red Pencils** and **Green Pencils** for saying special things in blue and red and green. And all these lovely things were in little pockets of their own in a Special Case which shut with a click when you clicked it. And they were all for Pooh.

'Oh!' said Pooh.

'Oh, Pooh!' said everybody else except Eeyore.

'Thank-you,' growled Pooh.

81

But Eeyore was saying to himself, 'This writing business. Pencils and what-not. Over-rated, if you ask me. Silly stuff. Nothing in it.'

Later on, when they had all said 'Good-bye' and 'Thank-you' to Christopher Robin, Pooh and Piglet walked home thoughtfully together in the golden evening, and for a long time they were silent.

'When you wake up in the morning, Pooh,' said Piglet at last, 'what's the first thing you say to yourself?'

'What's for breakfast?' said Pooh. 'What do *you* say, Piglet?'

'I say, I wonder what's going to happen exciting *to-day?*' said Piglet.

Pooh nodded thoughtfully.
'It's the same thing,' he said.

* * *

'And what did happen?' asked Christoper Robin.
'When?'
'Next morning.'
'I don't know.'
'Could you think, and tell me and Pooh sometime?'
'If you wanted it very much.'
'Pooh does,' said Christopher Robin.

He gave a deep sigh, picked his bear up by the leg and walked off to the door, trailing Winnie-the-Pooh behind him. At the door he turned and said, 'Coming to see me have my bath?'
'I might,' I said.
'Was Pooh's pencil case any better than mine?'
'It was just the same,' I said.
He nodded and went out . . . and

83

behind him.

the stairs

bump — going up

bump, bump,

Winnie - the -Pooh —

in a moment I heard

Journey's End

Christopher, Christopher, where are you going,
Christopher Robin?
'Just up to the top of the hill,
Upping and upping until

I am right on the top of the hill,'

Said Christopher Robin.

Christopher, Christopher, why are you going,
Christopher Robin?
There's nothing to see, so when
You've got to the top, what then?

'Just down to the bottom again,'

Said Christopher Robin.

Us Two

Wherever I am, there's always Pooh,
There's always Pooh and Me.
Whatever I do, he wants to do,
'Where are you going to-day?' says Pooh:
'Well, that's very odd 'cos I was too.
'Let's go together,' says Pooh, says he.
'Let's go together,' says Pooh.

'What's twice eleven?' I said to Pooh.
('Twice what?' said Pooh to Me.)
'I *think* it ought to be twenty-two.'
'Just what I think myself,' said Pooh.
'It wasn't an easy sum to do,
But that's what it is,' said Pooh, said he.
'That's what it is,' said Pooh.

'Let's look for dragons,' I said to Pooh.
'Yes, let's,' said Pooh to Me.
We crossed the river and found a few –
'Yes, those are dragons all right,' said Pooh.
'As soon as I saw their beaks I knew.
That's what they are,' said Pooh, said he.
'That's what they are,' said Pooh.

'Let's frighten the dragons,' I said to Pooh.
'That's right,' said Pooh to Me.
'*I'm* not afraid,' I said to Pooh,
And I held his paw and shouted 'Shoo!
Silly old dragons!' – and off they flew.
'I wasn't afraid,' said Pooh, said he,
'I'm *never* afraid with you.'

So wherever I am, there's always Pooh,
There's always Pooh and Me.
'What would I do?' I said to Pooh,
'If it wasn't for you,' and Pooh said: 'True,
It isn't much fun for One, but Two
Can stick together,' says Pooh, says he.
'That's how it is,' says Pooh.

Sneezles

Christopher Robin
Had wheezles
And sneezles,
They bundled him
Into
His bed.
They gave him what goes
With a cold in the nose,
And some more for a cold
In the head.

They wondered
If wheezles
Could turn
Into measles,
If sneezles
Would turn
Into mumps;

They examined his chest
For a rash,
And the rest
Of his body for swellings and lumps.
They sent for some doctors
In sneezles
And wheezles
To tell them what ought
To be done.

All sorts and conditions
Of famous physicians
Came hurrying round
At a run.
They all made a note
Of the state of his throat,

They asked if he suffered from thirst;
They asked if the sneezles
Came *after* the wheezles,
Or if the first sneezle
Came first.
They said, 'If you teazle
A sneezle
Or wheezle,
A measle
May easily grow.
But humour or pleazle
The wheezle
Or sneezle,
The measle
Will certainly go.'

They expounded the reazles
For sneezles
And wheezles,
The manner of measles
When new.
They said 'If he freezles
In draughts and in breezles,
Then **Phtheezles**
May even ensue.'

Christopher Robin
Got up in the morning,
The sneezles had vanished away.
And the look in his eye
Seemed to say to the sky,
'*Now, how to amuse them to-day?*'

The Friend

There are lots and lots of people who are always asking
    things,
Like Dates and Pounds-and-ounces and the names of funny
    Kings,
And the answer's either Sixpence or A Hundred Inches
    Long,
And I know they'll think me silly if I get the answer
    wrong.

So Pooh and I go whispering, and Pooh looks very bright,
And says, 'Well, *I* say sixpence, but I don't suppose I'm
    right.'
And then it doesn't matter what the answer ought to be,
'Cos if he's right, I'm Right, and if he's wrong, it isn't Me.

Rabbit's Busy Day

(In which Rabbit has a busy day, and we learn
what Christopher Robin does in the mornings)

It was going to be one of Rabbit's busy days. As soon as he woke up he felt important, as if everything depended upon him. It was just the day for Organizing Something, or for Writing a Notice Signed Rabbit, or for Seeing What Everybody Else Thought About It. It was a perfect morning for hurrying round to Pooh, and saying, 'Very well, then, I'll tell Piglet,' and then going to Piglet, and saying, 'Pooh thinks – but perhaps I'd better see Owl first.'

It was a Captainish sort of day, when everybody said, 'Yes, Rabbit' and 'No, Rabbit,' and waited until he had told them.

He came out of his house and sniffed the warm spring morning as he wondered what he would do. Kanga's house was nearest, and at Kanga's house was Roo, who said **'Yes, Rabbit'** and **'No, Rabbit'** almost better than anybody else in the Forest; but there was another animal there nowadays, the strange and Bouncy Tigger;

and he was the sort of Tigger who was always in front when you were showing him the way anywhere,

and was generally out of sight when at last you came to the place and said proudly, **'Here we are!'**

'No, not Kanga's,' said Rabbit thoughtfully to himself, as he curled his whiskers in the sun; and, to make quite sure that he wasn't going there, he turned to the left and trotted off in the other direction, which was the way to Christopher Robin's house.

'After all,' said Rabbit to himself,

'Christopher Robin depends on Me.

100

He's fond of Pooh and Piglet and Eeyore, and so am I, but they haven't any Brain. Not to notice. And he respects Owl, because you can't help respecting anybody who can spell TUESDAY, even if he doesn't spell it right; but spelling isn't everything. There are days when spelling Tuesday simply doesn't count. And Kanga is too busy looking after Roo, and Roo is too young and Tigger is too bouncy to be of any help, so there's really nobody but Me, when you come to look at it. I'll go and see if there's anything he wants doing, and then I'll do it for him. It's just the day for doing things.'

He trotted along happily, and by-and-by he crossed the stream and came to the place where his friends-and-relations lived. There seemed to be even more of them about than usual this morning, and having nodded to a hedgehog or two, with whom he was too busy to shake hands and having said,

'Good morning, good morning,'

importantly to some of the others, and 'Ah, there you are,' kindly, to the smaller ones, he waved a paw at them over his shoulder, and was gone;

101

leaving such an air of excitement and I-don't-know-what behind him, that several members of the Beetle family, including Henry Rush, made their way at once to the Hundred Acre Wood and began climbing trees, in the hope of getting to the top before it happened, whatever it was, so that they might see it properly.

Rabbit hurried on by the edge of the Hundred Acre Wood, feeling more important every minute, and soon he came to the tree where Christopher Robin lived.

He knocked at the door, and he called out once or twice, and then he walked back a little way and put his paw up to keep the sun out, and called to the top of the tree, and then he turned all round and shouted **'Hallo!'** and **'I say!' 'It's Rabbit!'** – but nothing happened.

Then he stopped and listened, and everything stopped and listened with him, and the Forest was very lone and still and peaceful in the sunshine, until suddenly a hundred miles above him a lark began to sing.

'Bother!' said Rabbit. 'He's gone out.'

He went back to the green front door, just to make sure, and he was turning away, feeling that his morning had got all spoilt, when he saw a piece of paper on the ground. And there was a pin in it, as if it had fallen off the door.

'Ha!' said Rabbit, feeling quite happy again. 'Another notice!'

This is what it said:

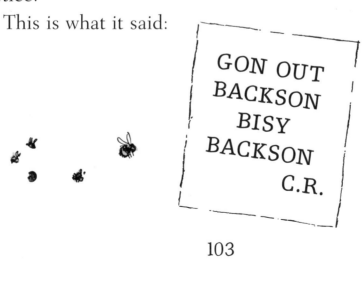

GON OUT
BACKSON
BISY
BACKSON
C.R.

'Ha!' said Rabbit again. 'I must tell the others.' And he hurried off importantly.

The nearest house was Owl's, and to Owl's House in the Hundred Acre Wood he made his way. He came to Owl's door, and he **knocked** and he **rang,** and he **rang** and he **knocked,** and at last Owl's head came out and said, 'Go away, I'm thinking – oh, it's you?' which was how he always began.

'Owl,' said Rabbit shortly, 'you and I have brains. The others have fluff.

If there is any thinking to be done in this Forest – and when I say thinking I mean *thinking* – you and I must do it.'

'Yes,' said Owl. 'I was.'

'Read that.'

Owl took Christopher Robin's notice from Rabbit and looked at it nervously. He could spell his own name **WOL,** and he could spell Tuesday so that you knew it wasn't Wednesday, and he could read quite comfortably when you weren't looking over his shoulder and saying 'Well?' all the time, and he could –

'Well?' said Rabbit.

'Yes,' said Owl, looking Wise and Thoughtful. 'I see what you mean. Undoubtedly.'

'Well?'

'Exactly,' said Owl. **'Precisely.'**

105

And he added, after a little thought, 'If you had not come to me, I should have come to you.'

'Why?' asked Rabbit.

'For that very reason,' said Owl, hoping that something helpful would happen soon.

'Yesterday morning,' said Rabbit solemnly, 'I went to see Christopher Robin. He was out. Pinned on his door was a notice!'

'The same notice?'

'A different one. But the meaning was the same. It's very odd.'

'Amazing,' said Owl, looking at the notice again, and getting, just for a moment, a curious sort of feeling that something had happened to Christopher Robin's back. 'What did you do?'

'Nothing.'

'The best thing,' said Owl wisely.

'Well?' said Rabbit again, as Owl knew he was going to.

'Exactly,' said Owl.

For a little while he couldn't think of anything more; and then, all of a sudden, he had an idea.

'Tell me, Rabbit,' he said, 'the *exact* words of the first notice. This is very important. Everything depends on this. The *exact* words of the *first* notice.'

'It was just the same as that one really.'

Owl looked at him, and wondered whether to push him off the tree; but, feeling that he could always do it afterwards, he tried once more to find out what they were talking about.

'The exact words, please,' he said, as if Rabbit hadn't spoken.

'It just said, **"Gon out. Backson."** Same as this, only this says **"Bisy Backson"** too.'

Owl gave a great sigh of relief.

'Ah!' said Owl. '*Now* we know where we are.'

'Yes, but where's Christopher Robin?' said Rabbit. 'That's the point.'

Owl looked at the notice again. To one of his education the reading of it was easy. 'Gon out, Backson. Bisy, Backson' – just the sort of thing you'd expect to see on a notice.

'It is quite clear what has happened, my dear Rabbit,' he said.

'Christopher Robin has gone out somewhere with Backson. He and Backson are busy together. Have you seen a Backson anywhere about in the Forest lately?'

'I don't know,' said Rabbit. 'That's what I came to ask you. What are they like?'

'Well,' said Owl, 'the Spotted or Herbaceous Backson is just a –'

'At least,' he said, 'it's really more of a –'

'Of course,' he said, 'it depends on the –'

'Well,' said Owl, 'the fact is,' he said, 'I don't know *what* they're like,' said Owl frankly.

'Thank you,' said Rabbit. And he hurried off to see Pooh.

Before he had gone very far he heard a noise. So he stopped and listened. This was the noise:

108

NOISE, BY POOH

Oh, the butterflies are flying,
Now the winter days are dying,
And the primroses are trying
    To be seen.
And the turtle-doves are cooing,
And the woods are up and doing,
For the violets are blue-ing
    In the green.

Oh, the honey-bees are gumming
On their little wings, and humming
That the summer, which is coming,
    Will be fun.
And the cows are almost cooing,
And the turtle-doves are mooing,
Which is why a Pooh is poohing
    In the sun.

109

For the spring is really springing;
You can see a skylark singing,
And the blue-bells, which are ringing,
    Can be heard.
And the cuckoo isn't cooing,
But he's cucking and he's ooing,
And a Pooh is simply poohing
    Like a bird.

'Hallo, Pooh,' said Rabbit.

'Hallo, Rabbit,' said Pooh dreamily.

'Did you make that song up?'

'Well, I sort of made it up,' said Pooh. 'It isn't Brain,' he went on humbly, 'because You Know Why, Rabbit; but it comes to me sometimes.'

'Ah!' said Rabbit, who never let things come to him, but always went and fetched them. 'Well, the point is, have you seen a Spotted or Herbaceous Backson in the Forest, at all?'

'No,' said Pooh. 'Not a – no,' said Pooh. 'I saw Tigger just now.'

'That's no good.'

'No,' said Pooh. 'I thought it wasn't.'

'Have you seen Piglet?'

'Yes,' said Pooh. 'I suppose *that* isn't any good either?' he asked meekly.

'Well, it depends if he saw anything.'

'He saw me,' said Pooh.

Rabbit sat down on the ground next to Pooh, and, feeling much less important like that, stood up again.

'What it all comes to is this,' he said,

'What does Christopher Robin do in the morning nowadays?'

'What sort of thing?'

'Well, can you tell me anything you've seen him do in the morning? These last few days.'

'Yes,' said Pooh. 'We had breakfast together yesterday. By the Pine Trees.

I'd made up a little basket, just a little, fair-sized basket, an ordinary biggish sort of basket, full of –'

'Yes, yes,' said Rabbit, 'but I mean later than that. Have you seen him between eleven and twelve?'

'Well,' said Pooh, 'at eleven o'clock – at eleven o'clock – well, at eleven o'clock, you see, I generally get home about then. Because I have One or Two Things to Do.'

'Quarter past eleven, then?'

'Well –' said Pooh.

'Half past?'

'Yes,' said Pooh. 'At half past –
or perhaps later – I might see him.'

And **now** that he did **think** of it,
he began **to remember** that
he hadn't seen Christopher Robin
about so much **lately.**

Not in the mornings. Afternoons, yes; evenings, yes;
before breakfast, yes; just after breakfast, yes. And then,
perhaps, 'See you again, Pooh,' and off he'd go.

'That's just it,' said Rabbit. 'Where?'

'Perhaps he's looking for something.'

'What?' asked Rabbit.

'That's just what I was going to say,'
said Pooh. And then he added, 'Perhaps
he's looking for a – for a –

'A **Spotted** or **Herbaceous**
Backson?'

'Yes,' said Pooh. 'One of those.

114

In case it isn't.'

Rabbit looked at him severely.

'I don't think you're helping,' he said.

'No,' said Pooh. 'I do try,' he added humbly.

Rabbit thanked him for trying, and said that he would now go and see Eeyore, and Pooh could walk with him if he liked. But Pooh, who felt another verse of his song coming on him, said he would wait for Piglet, good-bye, Rabbit; so Rabbit went off.

But, as it happened, it was Rabbit who saw Piglet first. Piglet had got up early that morning to pick himself a bunch of violets; and when he had picked them and put them in a pot in the middle of his house, it suddenly came over him that nobody had ever picked Eeyore a bunch of violets, and the more he thought of this, the more he thought how sad it was to be an Animal who had never had a bunch of violets picked for him.

So he hurried out again, saying to himself, 'Eeyore, Violets,' and then, 'Violets, Eeyore,' in case he forgot, because it was that sort of day, and he picked a large bunch and trotted along, smelling them, and feeling very happy, until he came to the place where Eeyore was.

'Oh, Eeyore,' began Piglet a little nervously, because Eeyore was busy.

Eeyore put out a paw and waved him away.

'To-morrow,' said Eeyore. 'Or the next day.'

Piglet came a little closer to see what it was. Eeyore had three sticks on the ground, and was looking at them. Two of the sticks were touching at one end, but not at the other, and the third stick was laid across them. Piglet

thought that perhaps it was a Trap of some kind.

'Oh, Eeyore,' he began again, 'I just –'

'Is that little Piglet?' said Eeyore, still looking hard at his sticks.

'Yes, Eeyore, and I –'

'Do you know what this is?'

'No,' said Piglet.

'It's an **A.'**

'Oh,' said Piglet.

'Not **O – A,'** said Eeyore severely. 'Can't you *hear*, or do you think you have more education than Christopher Robin?'

'Yes,' said Piglet. 'No,' said Piglet very quickly. And he came closer still.

'Christopher Robin said it was an **A,** and an **A** it is – until somebody treads on it,' Eeyore added sternly.

Piglet jumped backwards hurriedly, and smelt at his violets.

'Do you know what **A** means, little Piglet?'

'No, Eeyore, I don't.'

'It means Learning, it means Education, it means all the things that you and Pooh haven't got. That's what **A** means.'

'Oh,' said Piglet again. 'I mean, does it?' he explained quickly.

'I'm telling you. People come and go in this Forest, and they say, "It's only Eeyore, so it doesn't count." They walk to and fro saying, "Ha-ha!" But do they know anything about **A?** They don't. It's just three sticks to *them*. But to the Educated – mark this, little Piglet – to the Educated, not meaning Poohs and Piglets, it's a great and glorious **A.** Not,' he added, 'just something that anybody can come and *breathe* on.'

Piglet stepped back nervously, and looked round for help.

'Here's Rabbit,' he said gladly. 'Hallo, Rabbit.'

Rabbit came up importantly, nodded to Piglet, and said, 'Ah, Eeyore,' in the voice of one who would be saying 'Good-bye' in about two more minutes.

'There's just one thing I wanted to ask you, Eeyore. What happens to Christopher Robin in the mornings nowadays?'

'What's this that I'm looking at?' said Eeyore still looking at it.

'Three sticks,' said Rabbit promptly.

'You see?' said Eeyore to Piglet. He turned to Rabbit.

118

'I will now answer your question,' he said solemnly.
'Thank you,' said Rabbit.

'What does Christopher Robin do in the mornings? He learns. He becomes Educated. He instigorates –

I *think* that is the word he mentioned, but I may be referring to something else – he instigorates **Knowledge.** In my small way I also, if I have the word right, am – am doing what he does. That, for instance, is –'

'An **A,**' said Rabbit, 'but not a very good one. Well, I must get back and tell the others.'

Eeyore looked at his sticks and then he looked at Piglet.

'What did Rabbit say it was?' he asked.

'An **A**,' said Piglet.

'Did you tell him?'

'No, Eeyore, I didn't. I expect he just knew.'

'He *knew*? You mean this **A** thing is a thing *Rabbit* knew?'

'Yes, Eeyore. He's clever, Rabbit is.'

'Clever!' said Eeyore scornfully, putting a foot heavily on

his three sticks. 'Education!' said Eeyore bitterly, jumping on his six sticks. 'What *is* Learning?' asked Eeyore as he kicked his twelve sticks into the air. 'A thing *Rabbit* knows! Ha!'

'I think –' began Piglet nervously.

'Don't,' said Eeyore.

'I think *Violets* are rather nice,' said Piglet. And he laid his bunch in front of Eeyore and scampered off.

* * *

Next morning the notice on Christopher Robin's door said:

GONE OUT
BACK SOON

C.R.

Which is why all the animals in the Forest – except, of course, the Spotted and Herbaceous Backson – now know what Christopher Robin does in the mornings.

Vespers

Little Boy kneels at the foot of the bed,
Droops on the little hands little gold head.
Hush! Hush! Whisper who dares!
Christopher Robin is saying his prayers.

God bless Mummy. I know that's right.
Wasn't it fun in the bath to-night?
The cold's so cold, and the hot's so hot.
Oh! *God bless Daddy* – I quite forgot.

122

If I open my fingers a little bit more,
I can see Nanny's dressing-gown on the door.
It's a beautiful blue, but it hasn't a hood.
Oh! *God bless Nanny and make her good.*

Mine has a hood, and I lie in bed,
And pull the hood right over my head,
And I shut my eyes, and I curl up small,
And nobody knows that I'm there at all.

Oh! *Thank you, God, for a lovely day.*
And what was the other I had to say?
I said 'Bless Daddy,' so what can it be?
Oh! Now I remember it. *God bless Me.*

Little Boy kneels at the foot of the bed,
Droops on the little hands little gold head.
Hush! Hush! Whisper who dares!
Christopher Robin is saying his prayers.

An Enchanted Place

(In which Christopher Robin and Pooh come to an enchanted place, and we leave them there)

Christopher Robin was going away. Nobody knew why he was going; nobody knew where he was going; indeed, nobody even knew why he knew that Christopher Robin *was* going away. But somehow or other everybody in the Forest felt that it was happening at last. Even Smallest-of-all, a friend-and-relation of Rabbit's who thought he had once seen Christopher Robin's foot, but couldn't quite be sure because perhaps it was something else, even S. of A. told himself that **Things were going to be Different;** and Late and Early, two other friends-and-relations, said, 'Well, Early?' and 'Well, Late?' to each other in such a hopeless sort of way that it really didn't seem any good waiting for the answer.

One day when he felt that he couldn't wait any longer, Rabbit brained out a Notice, and this is what it said:

'Notice a **meeting** of everybody will meet at the House at Pooh Corner to pass a Rissolution By Order Keep to the Left Signed Rabbit.'

He had to write this out two or three times before he could get the rissolution to look like what he thought it was going to when he began to spell it; but, when at last it was finished, he took it round to everybody and read it out to them. And they all said they would come.

'Well,' said Eeyore that afternoon, when he saw them all walking up to his house, 'this *is* a surprise. Am *I* asked too?'

'Don't mind Eeyore,' whispered Rabbit to Pooh. 'I told him all about it this morning.'

Everybody said 'How-do-you-do' to Eeyore, and Eeyore said that he didn't, not to notice, and then they sat down;

and as soon as they were all sitting down, Rabbit stood up again.

'We all know why we're here,' he said, 'but I have asked my friend Eeyore –'

'That's Me,' said Eeyore. 'Grand.'

'I have asked him to Propose a Rissolution.' And he sat down again. 'Now then, Eeyore,' he said.

'Don't Bustle me,' said Eeyore, getting up slowly. 'Don't now-then me.' He took a piece of paper from behind his ear, and unfolded it. 'Nobody knows anything about this,' he went on. 'This is a Surprise.' He coughed in an important way, and began again: **'What-nots and Etceteras,** before I begin, or perhaps I should say,

before I end, I have a piece of Poetry to read to you. Hitherto – hitherto – a long word meaning – well, you'll see what it means directly – hitherto, as I was saying,

all the Poetry in the Forest

has been written by Pooh,

a Bear with a Pleasing Manner

but a Positively Startling

Lack of Brain.

The Poem which I am now about to read to you was written by Eeyore, or Myself, in a Quiet Moment. If somebody will take Roo's bull's-eye away from him, and wake up Owl, we shall all be able to enjoy it. I call it – POEM.'

This was it:

Christopher Robin is going.
At least I think he is.
Where
Nobody knows.
But he is going –
I mean he goes
(To rhyme with 'knows')
Do we care?
(To rhyme with 'where')
We do
Very much.
(I haven't got a rhyme for that
'is' in the second line yet.
Bother.)
(Now I haven't got a rhyme for
bother. Bother.)
Those two bothers will have
to rhyme with each other
Buther.
The fact is this is more difficult

than I thought,
I ought –
(Very good indeed)
I ought
To begin again,
But it is easier
To stop.
Christopher Robin, good-bye,
I
(Good)
I
And all your friends
Sends –
I mean all your friend
Send –
*(Very awkward this, it keeps
    going wrong.)*
Well, anyhow, we send
Our love
END.

'If anybody wants to clap,' said Eeyore when he had read this, 'now is the time to do it.'

They all clapped.

'Thank you,' said Eeyore. 'Unexpected and gratifying, if a little lacking in Smack.'

'It's much better than mine,' said Pooh admiringly, and he really thought it was.

'Well,' explained Eeyore modestly, 'it was meant to be.'

'The rissolution,' said Rabbit, 'is that we all sign it, and take it to Christopher Robin.'

So it was signed **PooH, WOL, PIGLET, EOR, RABBIT, KANGA, BLOT, SMUDGE,** and they all went off to Christopher Robin's house with it.

'Hallo, everybody,' said Christopher Robin – 'Hallo, Pooh.'

They all said 'Hallo,' and felt awkward and unhappy suddenly, because it was a sort of good-bye they were saying, and they didn't want to think about it. So they stood around, and waited for somebody else to speak, and they nudged each other, and said 'Go on,' and gradually Eeyore was nudged to the front, and the others crowded behind him.

'What is it, Eeyore?' asked Christopher Robin.

Eeyore swished his tail from side to side, so as to encourage himself, and began.

'Christopher Robin,' he said, 'we've come to say – to give you – it's called – written by – but we've all – because we've heard, I mean we all know – well, you see, it's – we – you – well, that, to put it as shortly as possible, is what it is.' He turned round angrily on the others and said, 'Everybody crowds round so in this Forest. There's no Space. I never saw a more Spreading lot of animals in my life, and all in the wrong places. Can't you

134

see that Christopher Robin wants to be alone? I'm going.'
And he humped off.

Not quite knowing why, the others began edging
away, and when Christopher Robin had finished reading
POEM, and was looking up to say 'Thank you,' only Pooh
was left.

It's a comforting sort of thing to have,'
said Christopher Robin,

folding up the paper, and putting it in his pocket. 'Come
on, Pooh,' and he walked off quickly.

'Where are we going?' said
Pooh, hurrying after him,

and wondering whether it was to be an Explore or a What-shall-I-do-about-you-know-what.

'**Nowhere,**' said Christopher Robin.

So they began going there, and after they had walked a little way Christopher Robin said:

'What do you like doing best in the world, Pooh?'

'Well,' said Pooh, 'what I like best –' and then he had to stop and think. Because although **Eating Honey** *was* a very good thing to do, there was a moment just before you began to eat it which was better than when you were, but he didn't know what it was called. And then he thought that being with Christopher Robin was a very good thing to do, and having Piglet near was a very friendly thing to have; and so, when he had thought it all out, he said, 'What I like best in the whole world is Me and Piglet going to see You, and You saying, "What about a little something?" and Me saying, "Well, I shouldn't mind a little something, should you, Piglet," and it being a hummy sort of day outside, and birds singing.'

'I like that too,' said Christopher Robin,

'but what I like *doing* best is **Nothing.**'

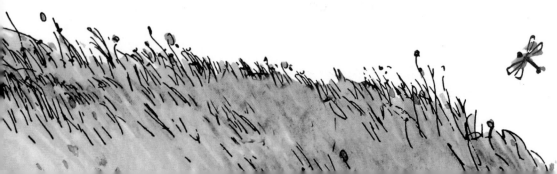

'How do you do Nothing?' asked Pooh, after he had wondered for a long time.

'Well, it's when people call out at you just as you're going off to do it, "What are you going to do, Christopher Robin?" and you say, "Oh, nothing," and then you go and do it.'

'Oh, I see,' said Pooh.

'This is a nothing sort of thing that we're doing now.'

'Oh, I see,' said Pooh again.

'It means just going along, listening to all the things you can't hear, and not bothering.'

'Oh!' said Pooh.

They walked on, thinking of This and That, and by-and-by they came to an enchanted place

on the very top of the Forest called Galleons Lap, which is sixty-something trees in a circle; and Christopher Robin knew that it was enchanted because nobody had

139

ever been able to count whether it was **63** or **64**, not even when he tied a piece of string round each tree after he had counted it. Being enchanted, its floor was not like the floor of the Forest, gorse and bracken and heather, but close-set grass, quiet and smooth and green. It was the only place in the Forest where you could sit down carelessly, without getting up again almost at once and looking for somewhere else. Sitting there they could see the whole world spread out until it reached the sky, and whatever there was all the world over was with them in Galleons Lap.

Suddenly Christopher Robin began to tell Pooh about some of the things:

People called Kings and Queens
and something called Factors,
and a place called Europe,
and an island in the middle of the
sea where no ships came,
and how you make a Suction Pump
(if you want to),
and when Knights were Knighted,
and what comes from Brazil.

And Pooh, his back against one of the sixty-something trees, and his paws folded in front of him, said 'Oh!' and 'I don't know,' and thought how wonderful it would be to have a Real Brain which could tell you things. And by-and-by Christopher Robin came to an end of the things, and was silent, and he sat there looking out over the world, and wishing it wouldn't stop.

But Pooh was thinking too, and he said suddenly to Christopher Robin:

'Is it a very Grand thing to be an Afternoon, what you said?'

'A what?' said Christopher Robin lazily, as he listened to something else.

'On a horse?' explained Pooh.

'A Knight?'

'Oh, was that it?' said Pooh. 'I thought it was a – Is it as Grand as a King and Factors and all the other things you said?'

'Well, it's not as grand as a King,' said Christopher Robin, and then, as Pooh seemed disappointed, he added quickly, 'but it's grander than Factors.'

'Could a Bear be one?'

'Of course he could!' said Christopher Robin. 'I'll make you one.' And he took a stick and touched Pooh on the shoulder, and said,

'Rise,
Sir Pooh de Bear,
most faithful
of all my
Knights.'

So Pooh rose and sat down and said 'Thank you,' which is the proper thing to say when you have been made a Knight, and he went into a dream again, in which he and Sir Pump and Sir Brazil and Factors lived together with a horse, and were faithful knights (all except Factors, who looked after the horse) to Good King Christopher Robin . . . and every now and then he shook his head, and said to himself, 'I'm not getting it right.' Then he began to think of all the things Christopher Robin would want to tell him when he came back from wherever he was going to, and how muddling it would be for a Bear of Very Little Brain to try and get them right in his mind. 'So, perhaps,' he said sadly to himself, 'Christopher Robin won't tell me any more,' and he wondered if being a Faithful Knight meant that you just went on being faithful without being told things.

Then, suddenly again, Christopher Robin, who was still looking at the world with his chin in his hands, called out, 'Pooh!'

'Yes?' said Pooh.

'When I'm – when – Pooh!'

'Yes, Christopher Robin?'

'I'm not going to do **Nothing** any more.'

'Never again?'
'Well, not so much. They don't let you.'
Pooh waited for him to go on, but he was silent again.
'Yes, Christopher Robin?' said Pooh helpfully.

'Pooh, when I'm – *you* know –
when I'm *not* doing Nothing,
will you come up here sometimes?'

'Just Me?'
'Yes, Pooh.'

'Will you be here too?'

'Yes, Pooh, I will be really. I *promise* I will be, Pooh.'

'That's good,' said Pooh.

'Pooh, *promise* you won't forget about me, ever. Not even when I'm a hundred.'

Pooh thought for a little.

'How old shall *I* be then?'

'Ninety-nine.'

Pooh nodded.

'I promise,' he said.

Still with his eyes on the world, Christopher Robin put out a hand and felt for Pooh's paw.

'Pooh,' said Christopher Robin earnestly, 'if I – if I'm not quite –' he stopped and tried again – 'Pooh, *whatever* happens, you *will* understand, won't you?'

'Understand what?'

'Oh, nothing.' He laughed and jumped to his feet. 'Come on!'

'Where?' said Pooh.

'Anywhere,' said Christopher Robin.

* * *

So they went off together.
But wherever they go,
and whatever happens to them on the way,
in that enchanted place
on the top of the Forest
a little boy and his Bear
will always be playing.

In the Dark

I've had my supper,
  And *had* my supper,
    And *HAD* my supper and all;
I've heard the story
  Of Cinderella,
    And how she went to the ball;
I've cleaned my teeth,
  And I've said my prayers,
    And I've cleaned and said them right;
And they've all of them been
  And kissed me lots,
    They've all of them said 'Good-night.'

So – here I am in the dark alone,
  There's nobody here to see;
    I think to myself,
    I play to myself,
  And nobody knows what I say to myself;
Here I am in the dark alone,

What is it going to be?
I can think whatever I like to think,
I can play whatever I like to play,
I can laugh whatever I like to laugh,
    There's nobody here but me.

I'm talking to a rabbit . . .
    I'm talking to the sun . . .
I think I am a hundred –
    I'm one.
I'm lying in a forest . . .
    I'm lying in a cave . . .
I'm talking to a Dragon . . .
    I'm BRAVE.
I'm lying on my left side . . .
    I'm lying on my right . . .
I'll play a lot to-morrow . . .

        .   .   .   .

I'll think a lot to-morrow . . .

     . . . .

I'll laugh . . .

        a lot . . .

           to-morrow . . .

       (Heigh-ho!)

            Good-night.

The End

When I was **1**,
I had just begun.

When I was **2**,
I was nearly new.

When I was **3**,
I was hardly Me.

When I was **4**,
I was not much more.

When I was **5**,
I was just alive.

But now I am **6**, I'm as clever as clever.
So I think I'll be six now for ever and ever.